E HUT
Hutchins, Pat, 1942-
Tidy Titch

DATE DUE   **9714474**

TIDY
TITCH

TIDY TITCH

by PAT HUTCHINS

A Mulberry Paperback Book
New York

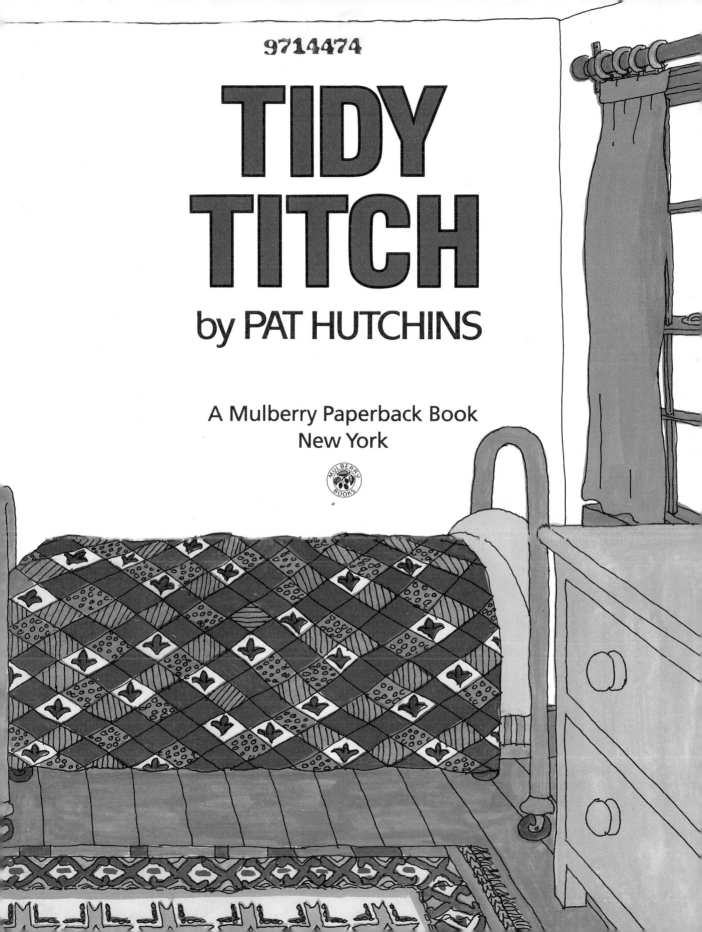

Watercolor paints and pen-and-ink were
used for the full-color art.
The text type is Mixage Medium.

The Library of Congress has cataloged the
Greenwillow Books edition of *Tidy Titch* as follows:
Hutchins, Pat. Tidy Titch / by Pat Hutchins. p. cm.
Summary: Titch helps his older brother
and sister clean their rooms.
ISBN 0-688-09963-7. ISBN 0-688-09964-5 (lib. bdg.)
[1. Cleanliness—Fiction. 2. Orderliness—Fiction.
3. Brothers and sisters—Fiction.] I. Title.
PZ7.H96165Th 1991 [E]—dc20 90-38483 CIP AC

5 7 9 10 8 6 4
First Mulberry Edition, 1994
ISBN 0-688-13648-6

FOR DAISY GOUNDRY

TIDY
TITCH

"How tidy Titch's room is,"
said Mother to Peter and Mary.
"And how messy your rooms are.
I think you should tidy them up."

"I'll help," said Titch
as Mother went downstairs.

"I think I'll throw this
   dollhouse out," said Mary,
"and these toys.
   I'm too old for them!"
"I'm not," said Titch.
"I'll have them!"

And Titch carried the dollhouse
and the toys to his room.

"I think I'll throw that old space suit out," said Peter, "and that cowboy outfit. They're much too small for me!"
"They're not too small for me!" said Titch. "I'll have them!"

And Titch carried the space suit
and the cowboy outfit to his room.

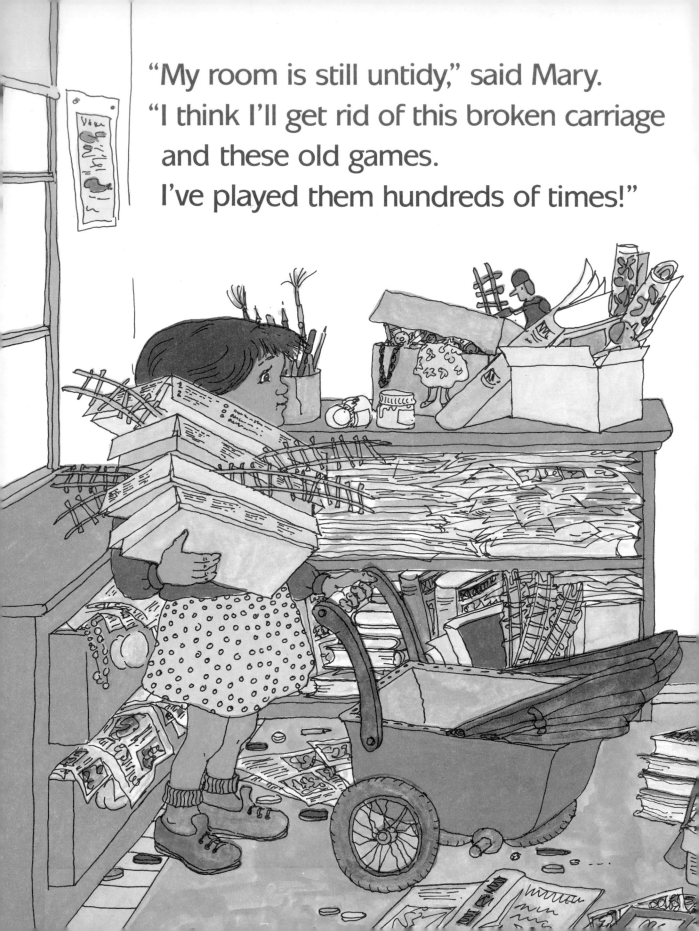

"My room is still untidy," said Mary.
"I think I'll get rid of this broken carriage
and these old games.
I've played them hundreds of times!"

"I haven't," said Titch.
"I'll have them!"

And Titch took the carriage
and old games to his room.

"My room is still a mess," said Peter.
"I think I'll get rid of
these old toys. I don't play
with them anymore!"
"I will!" said Titch.
"I'll have them!"

And Titch carried the old toys to his room.

"How neat your rooms are!" said Mother
when she came back upstairs.

"I thought Titch was going to help you."

"He did," said Peter and Mary.

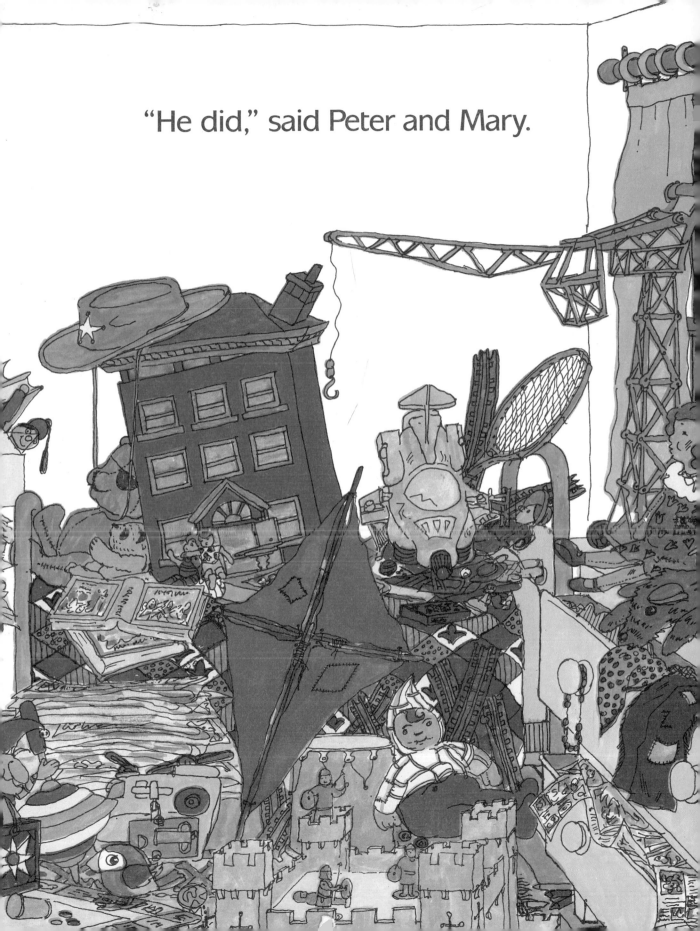

Since the publication of *Rosie's Walk* in 1968, reviewers on both sides of the Atlantic have been loud in their praise of Pat Hutchins's work.

Among her popular picture books are *What Game Shall We Play?*; *Where's the Baby?* (an *SLJ* Best Book of the Year); *The Doorbell Rang* (an ALA Notable Book); *You'll Soon Grow into Them, Titch*; and *The Wind Blew* (winner of the 1974 Kate Greenaway Medal). For older readers she has written several novels, including *The House That Sailed Away, The Curse of the Egyptian Mummy,* and *Rats!*

Pat Hutchins, her husband, Laurence, and their sons, Morgan and Sam, live in London, England.